WHOSE FOOTPRINTS?

WHOSE FOOTPRINTS?

BY MOLLY COXE

THOMAS Y. CROWELL   NEW YORK

For Will

Whose Footprints?
Copyright © 1990 by Molly Coxe
Printed in the U.S.A. All rights reserved.
Typography by Andrew Rhodes
1 2 3 4 5 6 7 8 9 10
First Edition

Library of Congress Cataloging-in-Publication Data
Coxe, Molly.
   Whose footprints? / Molly Coxe.
     p.   cm.
   Summary: A mother and daughter discover and identify animal footprints in the snow on an intimate walk through their farm.
   ISBN 0-690-04835-1 : $. — ISBN 0-690-04837-8 : $
   [1. Animal tracks—Fiction. 2. Mothers and daughters—Fiction.] I. Title.
PZ7.C839424Wk   1990   89-70850
[E]—dc20   CIP
                                                AC

Whose footprints?

Whose footprints?

The rooster's.

Whose footprints?

The sheep's.

Whose footprints?

The dog's!

Whose footprints?

And Daddy's!